THE LITTLE BOOK OF PET HATES

by

Michael J Vine

CONTENTS

INTRODUCTION

At the tender age of 52, I write this introduction to my very first book not knowing whether this will be of interest to anyone, or indeed if anyone will buy it!

This book is the result of an item included on my "Bucket List" of things to do in my life, so I am pleased that I can finally tick that one off now. And I am very proud of the results.

The initial challenge was to identify what to write a book about, and that in itself took over 5 years! But the 'eureka' moment finally arrived. My love of watching and listening to comedy, as well as my own attempts to try and be funny (which none of my three children think I am), helped me to realise that the funniest things in life are indeed the 'every day' things that occur.

I also realised that as I get older, my list of 'Pet Hates' has grown rapidly. I guess I could be considered a "Grumpy Old Man", but the items listed on the following pages don't make me cross or grumpy in any way (okay, one or two might), but they are just the small observations in life which can be mildly frustrating to me, and which I have learned to laugh about. I have learned that I cannot influence anyone else's behaviour in any way, and it literally 'is what it is'.

Definition of Pet Hate (aka Pet Aversion, Pet Peeve): *a minor annoyance that an individual identifies as irritating to them, to a greater degree than would be expected based on the experience of others*

So, this seemed the ideal subject to write about. I have listed various topics, and my Pet Hates for each of them. I hope you can relate to them, and maybe agree with some of them. But I have no doubt that it will make you stop and think about your experiences, and you will be able to add your own. Enjoy...

Aɪʀᴘᴏʀᴛs / Fʟʏɪɴɢ

❖ Having to get to the airport so many hours in advance of the flight

❖ Not being able to find a trolley to put your luggage on

❖ People getting in the way as you walk through the airport with your large suitcase

❖ Having to check the weight and size of your luggage, and realising that the weight machine at the airport has a different reading to your home scales

❖ Waiting and queuing for the Check In Desk to open

❖ A Check In queue blocking the walkway, and trying to find a gap to get through it

❖ Not enough Check In staff

❖ Unfriendly Check In staff

❖ Check In staff chatting to each other and oblivious to the queues waiting and growing

❖ Non user-friendly online Check In screens at airports

❖ When you are just over the luggage weight allocation, and there is no flexibility from the Check In staff

❖ When you have to take things out of your main suitcase at the airport in front of other people, and put them in your hand luggage, in order to avoid exceeding the maximum weight allowed, thus ensuring no additional luggage charges

❖ When you are in a queue behind people having to take things out of their main suitcase in order to meet the weight allocation

❖ When going through the Security Check, the people who don't read the signs to take off shoes, belts, any metal items before going through the scanners, and end up causing everyone else a delay

❖ The long walk to some Departure Gates

❖ People who request assistance from an Airport Buggy to get to the Departure Gate, when they really don't need it

❖ People who have to be first on the plane

❖ When the entire plane is waiting for one remaining passenger to board before it can commence the take-off process

- ❖ When you take your seat on the plane, look out of the window and see your suitcase being thrown into the hold

- ❖ When the largest person on the flight is in the seat next to you

- ❖ When the person sat next to you has body odour issues

- ❖ When you realise that there is a Stag / Hen Party on the flight, who have been drinking since arriving at the airport

- ❖ When the plane starts taxi-ing along the runway, and you suddenly need the toilet, and you are not sure how long you can wait

- ❖ When the person in front decides to recline their seat, even though there is hardly any space to do so

- ❖ When there is a long queue for the toilet

- ❖ When the person in the toilet in front of you is taking ages, and you are desperate

- ❖ When you are going to the toilet, and the plane hits turbulence

- ❖ When you want to return to your seat, and the Cabin Crew won't let you pass because they are busy serving dinner / drinks to passengers from their trolley

❖ People who snore on the flight

❖ People who have to be first to get off of the plane

❖ When you arrive at the Luggage Carousel, but cannot see anything as everyone is stood too close, and you just want to shout out "Everyone take two steps back" so that you can see

❖ When your suitcase is the last one off of the plane at the destination airport

❖ When you retrieve your suitcase and it has been damaged in transit

❖ When you don't retrieve your suitcase as it has been sent on another flight in error

❖ When you are expecting to be met at the airport and cannot locate the driver

❖ When the signs at the destination airport are not very clear

❖ Trying to find a toilet at the destination airport

Barbers / Hair Salon

❖ People who do not like the outcome of their haircut, but still leave a tip

❖ When you are in a barbers, and have to wait your turn, but the barber you want to cut your hair is busy with another customer, so you have to have someone new to cut your hair

❖ Awkward silences

❖ Not feeling in the mood to talk, but still going through the motions

❖ Pointless conversations with someone who is not interested

❖ Having your hairstyle request ignored by someone who thinks they know what is best for you

❖ Having more hair cut off than you wanted

❖ A hairdresser talking to you whilst the hairdryer is on, and you can't hear a thing

❖ Out of date magazines

❖ Not being offered a tea or coffee

❖ When you are offered a tea or coffee, and don't know if it is included in the price or chargeable

Beach

❖ People who don't put their litter in the bin, or take it home

❖ People who leave their used 'disposable' barbecues on the beach

❖ People who leave their litter on the beach, including glass bottles

❖ People who dig holes in the sand and leave them for others to fall into

❖ People who let their dogs on the "No Dogs" section of the beach

❖ Cyclists who think they own the promenade and get annoyed when somebody walks in front of them

❖ Cyclists who cycle too quickly when the promenade is packed with people

❖ Cyclists who ignore the signs saying "No Cycling" at specified times of the year

❖ Women walking along the promenade in just a bikini

❖ Over-sized women wearing thongs

❖ Over-sized men wearing just a pair of Speedo's

❖ Swimwear that becomes see-through when wet

❖ Middle-aged and old men walking along the promenade with no top on, and flaunting a beer belly

❖ People using beach umbrellas on windy days which aren't secured into the sand, and are then blown along the beach, endangering others

❖ When you carefully place your towel on the sand, and somebody runs past and kicks sand over you and your towel

❖ When you find the perfect quiet spot on the beach, lay your towel down, lay down and close your eyes, only to be woken by the 'family from hell'

❖ Amusement arcades where you win tickets which are then used to trade in for rubbish prizes

❖ Change machines in amusement arcades which are always empty

❖ Seagulls stealing food out of people's hands

❖ People who argue on the beach

- ❖ Parents shouting at their children

- ❖ Children shouting at their parents

- ❖ Groups who play games like football, volleyball and frisbee when the beach is full, and end up annoying others

- ❖ Getting sand on your sandwiches

- ❖ Drying off after a swim and the feeling of dry salt on the body

- ❖ Beach resorts which have a local version of the London Eye, yet there is little to see from it apart from sea and sand

- ❖ The fresh air of a lovely beach stroll being spoiled when walking past someone smoking pot/weed

- ❖ People walking into public conveniences with nothing on their feet

- ❖ People playing volleyball on a naturist beach; not a good look

- ❖ Buying an ice cream for your child, only to know that it will be dropped within seconds

CALL CENTRES

❖ Receiving a "cold call" from a call centre

❖ When you phone a call centre and get the options to press 1, 2 etc., and none of them fit exactly what you want

❖ When you phone a call centre and are then held in a queue for ages

❖ When you phone a call centre and are then held in a queue for ages, and don't know whether to hang up or not

❖ When on hold, and you get the messages that "All our operators are busy" and "Your call is important to us"

❖ When you cannot understand clearly what the person in the call centre is saying

❖ When you finally get to speak to someone at a call centre, but then you have run out of time to talk

❖ Overseas based call centres

❖ Insincere people receiving your calls

❖ When you speak to different people whenever you call

❖ When you finish the call and see how much time your have spent on the call

❖ When you finish the call and realise that there was another question that you needed to ask

❖ Knowing in advance that the whole process of phoning a call centre will be frustrating

CAR PARKING

❖ People who do not park correctly within the allocated parking bay

❖ Parking next to large 4x4 vehicles, and having to struggle to get out of your vehicle

❖ People who park in a disabled parking bay, but aren't disabled

❖ Car parks which have way too many disabled and parent/child spaces

❖ Car parks where the bays are so small that you have no option but to bang your car door on the neighbouring car in order to get out

❖ Car parks with very tight ramps to get up and down floors

❖ Queuing outside a car park for someone to leave before you can get parked

❖ Expensive car parks

❖ When you don't quite have enough change on you to pay for the time of stay that you require

❖ When not having enough change, the time taken to register to pay online, when you are in a rush

❖ Buying a ticket then realising that you didn't need to as it is free at the time you want

❖ When new 'hi tech' ticket machines are installed, and people do not understand how to use them

Chewing Gum / Bubble Gum

❖ People who spit their chewing gum onto the pavement

❖ Stepping on chewing gum which then sticks to the bottom of your shoe

❖ Spending ages trying to remove chewing gum from the bottom of your shoe

❖ That initial feeling when you have accidentally swallowed some chewing gum

❖ When the flavour of the chewing gum has gone

❖ People who leave chewing gum underneath a table or desk

❖ People who chew gum with their mouth open

❖ People who make too much noise when chewing gum

❖ People who blow bubbles with their gum

❖ The noise a bubble makes when it pops

CHILDREN

- ❖ Children being noisy

- ❖ Young children who have the ability to manipulate both of their parents simultaneously

- ❖ Children who swear

- ❖ Children who pick their nose in public

- ❖ Children who don't seem to know how to blow their nose

- ❖ Children who don't say please and thank you

- ❖ Children who demand sweets in the supermarket

- ❖ Children who say "I need..."

- ❖ Children who say "I want..."

- ❖ Children who let their parents down in front of others

- ❖ Children who have tantrums in public

- ❖ Children who cry unnecessarily

❖ Children who fake a cry to get their own way

❖ Children who do things they know they aren't meant to do

❖ Children who blame others when they have been naughty

Coffee Shops

❖ When you place an order for several drinks and the person behind the till can only remember the first drink of your order

❖ After placing your coffee order with the person at the till, and then having to repeat it again to the barista

❖ When you are asked if you want the more expensive "Premium Blend" of coffee, rather than the "Normal Blend"

❖ Staff who do not notice when there is a customer waiting to be served

❖ Staff who do not seem to care about providing a quality service

❖ Trainee baristas

❖ When all of the free newspapers are being read by others

❖ When people don't return the newspapers to the correct place

❖ When one person takes two newspapers, yet can only read one at a time

❖ When people take the coffee shop newspapers home

❖ When a customer has completed the crossword of the coffee shop newspaper

❖ When a customer rips out articles from the coffee shop newspaper

❖ When you miss the cut-off for the breakfast or lunchtime meal deal by a minute

❖ People who make one drink last for ages

❖ Crumbs left on the seats

❖ People who only go into the coffee shop to use the toilets

❖ When all of the tables still have used cups and plates on them

❖ When a person on their own takes up a large table when the coffee shop is really busy

Cyclists

- ❖ Cyclists who ring their bell unnecessarily

- ❖ Cyclists who ride with headphones or both earphones in

- ❖ Cyclists who ride two or more abreast on the road

- ❖ Cyclists who ride on a pavement even when there is a cycle lane on the road

- ❖ Cyclists with flashing halogen lights

- ❖ Cyclists who use their lights in the daytime

- ❖ Cyclists who wear Lycra, who don't really have the right body for it

- ❖ Cyclists who use an electric bike

- ❖ Electric bike cyclists who overtake push bike cyclists

- ❖ Cyclists who don't indicate when they are turning left or right

- ❖ Cyclists who ride "no handed" on a road

DIETING CLUBS

- ❖ Dieting clubs where the leader is larger than yourself

- ❖ Being told patronisingly how easy it is to lose weight

- ❖ The weigh in process

- ❖ Having to explain to a group of strangers why you put on weight, or how you lost weight

- ❖ Having to stay for an hour after weigh-in to listen to the leader talk about each attendee

- ❖ Being made to feel guilty if you don't stay for the class discussion after the weigh-in

- ❖ Having to record everything that you eat and drink in a diary, and being honest about it

- ❖ Holding back the desire to eat unhealthy food like chocolate

- ❖ Noticing what your friends and family are eating around you, and feeling that it all seems so unfair

- ❖ When your friends are always eating and drinking bad things, yet they are still slim

- ❖ Attending a function and not being able to partake in the lovely food provided

Doctors

❖ Doctors receptionists who make you feel that you are wasting their time

❖ Doctors receptionists who seem to believe that they are qualified doctors

❖ Doctors receptionists who make you feel that there is nothing wrong with you, even though you know there is

❖ When you phone for a quick appointment, and are told the earliest appointment is in two weeks' time

❖ When you arrive at the doctors for your appointment and the symptoms appear to have gone, but then reappear as soon as you leave

❖ Sitting in a waiting room surrounded by people who are coughing and spluttering

❖ Sitting in a waiting room for 30 minutes, and still knowing that there are others ahead of you in the queue

- ❖ When you want to discuss a sensitive issue with the doctor, and they have a student doctor with them

- ❖ When you take a prescription to the pharmacy and they don't have what you want in stock

FASHION

❖ People wearing three-quarter length cargo shorts with pockets

❖ People wearing three-quarter length tracksuit or shell suit trousers

❖ People wearing multiple brands of sportswear at the same time

❖ Partners wearing matching clothes and shoes

❖ Velour tracksuits

❖ Shell suits

❖ People copying what other people wear, but still claiming to have their own individual style

❖ People wearing "Crocs" shoes, apart from those in the medical profession

❖ People not wearing 'age appropriate' clothing

❖ People over the age of 20 wearing dungarees

❖ Young men wearing their trousers half way down their legs and showing their designer underwear

- ❖ Women who lean over and the top of their thong appears

- ❖ Young children with their ears pierced

- ❖ Socks with sandals

- ❖ Fake designer clothes

Football

❖ Football team replica shirts being worn by adults anywhere away from a match

❖ Fans who think they know better than the manager

❖ Fans always criticising rather than encouraging

❖ Fans who think football is the most important thing in life

❖ Drunk fans at matches

❖ Queues for refreshments and the toilets

❖ Fans who jump into you when your team has scored a goal

❖ Referees who spoil the game with their poor decision making

❖ Assistant referees who won't make a decision about which team has the throw in, and wait for the referee to indicate which way

❖ Players who cheat on the pitch, by diving for example

❖ Players not giving 100%

❖ Players who think they are bigger than the club

❖ Players who break their contract with a club

❖ Players who do not acknowledge their own fans outside the ground and give autographs or engage in conversation

❖ Football pundits who state the obvious

HEN AND STAG PARTIES

❖ Hen and Stag Parties wearing tacky t-shirts with slogans

❖ Hen and Stag Parties wearing ridiculous fancy dress outfits

❖ Hen and Stag Parties who include old people who don't want to be there and look out of place

❖ Old people on a Hen or Stag Party who think that they can keep up with the younger members

❖ Strippers being arranged for the bride-to-be or groom-to-be

❖ Tacky accessories, such as straws in phallic shapes

❖ When you are staying in the same hotel as a Hen or Stag Party

❖ When a Hen or Stag Party come into the pub that you are drinking in

❖ When you are part of a Hen or Stag Party, and are forced to drink the same amount as everyone else

❖ Being designated as the "kitty holder"

❖ Drinking games where the loser has to drink a cocktail of different spirits

❖ The morning after feeling...

❖ The morning after, and knowing that you have to do it all again the next day

❖ That the traditional Hen or Stag Night is now a Hen or Stag Week

LITTER

- ❖ People who throw litter on the streets

- ❖ People who throw litter out of their cars

- ❖ Litter left in parks and on beaches

- ❖ People who leave litter despite there being a bin close by

- ❖ Overflowing bins

- ❖ Dirty bins

- ❖ People putting the wrong things in the recycling bins

- ❖ People not rinsing out jars/bottles for recycling

- ❖ The Refuse Collection service returning the wrong bin to your house

- ❖ The Refuse Collection service dropping waste on the ground, and then leaving it

- ❖ Neighbours who put their rubbish into your bins without asking, because their bin is full

- ❖ Cigarette butts discarded on the ground as though it is acceptable

- ❖ Litter along the sides of roads

- ❖ Treading on litter

- ❖ Litter bins that seagulls can drag rubbish from, which then gets discarded everywhere

- ❖ People not realising the impact to the planet of not disposing of litter correctly

- ❖ People who do not realise that leaving litter everywhere actually costs the taxpayer

Motorways

❖ Middle lane drivers

❖ Motorists who drive too close to the vehicle in front

❖ When traffic is crawling along in all lanes, and you seem to be in the slowest lane

❖ Motorists who drive too slowly on a motorway

❖ Motorists overtaking at more than 100mph who never get stopped for speeding

❖ Where there are road works, and you never see anyone working, despite plenty of people on site

❖ Where there are roadworks and somebody is actually working, while so many other people are standing around watching

❖ When you are following road diversion signs, which suddenly stop

❖ When a roadwork diversion directs you to an alternate route that also has road works

- ❖ Forgetting that you have been driving in an Average Speed Check area and wondering if you have been going too fast

- ❖ When you catch up with lots of cars all sticking to the 70mph speed limit as there is a police car in the distance ahead, only to discover it is just a Highways Agency vehicle

- ❖ The time taken to create Smart motorways

- ❖ Driving through motorway roadworks at 50mph for mile after mile

PARENTING

❖ Feeling like you have to please everyone else

❖ Being the one to try and maintain the peace within the household

❖ Your children 'borrowing' your clothes / toiletries without asking

❖ Being taken for granted by your children

❖ Having to continually educate your children to do some chores, without having to ask them every time

❖ Dealing with children who always think they are right

❖ Dealing with children who are always moaning

❖ When a child lies, and thinks you won't know the real truth

❖ Children expecting their parents to run around after them, and not being grateful

❖ Children demanding the latest brands of clothing and phones

❖ Children playing off one parent against the other

- ❖ Children not appreciating the value of money

- ❖ Having to do things you do not want to

- ❖ Having to deal with family disputes, and family not talking to each other

- ❖ Dealing with the fallout of your child when they discover alcohol

- ❖ Dealing with the upset when your child's relationships come to an end

PEOPLE

- ❖ People who eat whilst they are walking

- ❖ People who talk with their mouth full

- ❖ People who throw litter

- ❖ People drinking alcohol in the streets

- ❖ People who spit on the streets

- ❖ People burping and making other noises in public

- ❖ People who walk past and knock into you

- ❖ People who ask you how you are, but don't listen to the response

- ❖ People who say to "Have a nice day!", but don't genuinely mean it

- ❖ People who don't say "Please" or "Thank you"

- ❖ People who don't acknowledge you when you say "Hello" to them

- ❖ People who don't acknowledge you, when you hold a door open for them

- ❖ People bragging about what they have

- ❖ People who talk endlessly about their children and how wonderful they are

- ❖ People who cannot handle their alcohol

- ❖ People who are too loud and spoil the atmosphere for everybody else

- ❖ People who ignore signs, like "Keep Off The Grass"

- ❖ People who do not pick up their Dog Litter

- ❖ People who always think they are right

- ❖ People serving you who greet you with an 'over the top' hello

- ❖ People who do not wash their hands after going to the toilet

- ❖ People who use mobility scooters but do not really need them and don't realise it is healthy to walk as much as possible

- ❖ People who use mobility scooters and ride them on the road

- ❖ People who seem to judge other people for choosing not to have children

- ❖ People who give their children weird names

- ❖ People who jump queues and push in

❖ People who shout right across you, to get someone else's attention

❖ People who go to church or change religion only to get their child into a specific school

❖ When you are in a group and buy a round of drinks, but every time you go out, it is the same friend that never buys a drink back

❖ Men with topknots

❖ Men with plaited beards

❖ Men with stretched ear lobe piercings

❖ Women who do not realise that they do not have the legs to go with a short skirt

❖ Overweight women who sit with their legs open and are wearing a skirt

❖ Old people who tell you their age as they want to hear the response "You don't look it"

❖ Old men not wearing a shirt in public places

❖ Men who walk around with their hands inside their trousers

Phones

❖ People spending too much time on their phones

❖ People who check their phones every 5 minutes, even though there has been no message alerts

❖ People who walk along the street looking at their phones and not being aware of other pedestrians

❖ People who have become so dependent upon their phones

❖ People who seem to have lost the old traditions of meeting up with friends and having face-to-face conversations

❖ People who walk along the street with their phone on loud speaker, meaning that you can hear their whole conversation

❖ People who have their ring-tones set at a high volume

❖ When you can hear other people's music despite them having earphones in

❖ People who create their own text jargon, which nobody understands

❖ People who go out for a meal with others, yet they all sit with their phones on the table constantly looking at them

Shopping

Supermarket

❖ When you always seem to select the shopping trolley with a dodgy wheel

❖ People who pick up an item, then later decide they don't want it so leave it wherever they are in the shop

❖ People who open food packets and eat whilst walking around the store, even though they have not yet paid for it

❖ Empty shelves

❖ When an item in the store has a "Best Before" date of today

❖ When people leave their trolleys across the aisle so that you can't get your trolley past them

❖ When the store layout is rearranged, and the products are moved to different aisles

❖ Long queues at tills

❖ People who take ages to load their shopping into bags

❖ When the Self Service till scanners are so sensitive that a member of staff has to intervene and reset the till after most of the items are scanned

❖ People who are too lazy to return their trolley to the trolley park after loading their car

DIY

❖ When DIY stores seem to have everything apart from the one item you want

❖ Trying to locate what you want within the store

❖ Trying to locate a trolley for the size of goods that you want to purchase

❖ People who have opened packaging to steal an item, and left the rest back on the shelf

Fashion

❖ When the size you want is the only one sold out

❖ When all sizes are mixed up on the racks and shelves

❖ Clothes shopping with someone who walks round and round the same shop so many times

❖ Trying to find a shop assistant in the Shoe section to get a pair of shoes for you to try

❖ Assistants too busy chatting to notice you

❖ When you get home and notice a small mark on your purchase

❖ Being asked when you pay if you want to take out a Store Card

❖ Being made to feel guilty for returning faulty goods

❖ When you want to exchange a faulty purchase, but there is no identical replacement available

SMOKING AND VAPING

❖ People throwing their cigarette butts onto the floor

❖ People flicking their cigarette ash out of a car window

❖ The smell of tobacco when a smoker walks past

❖ People who empty their car ashtray by the side of the road

❖ People with yellow/brown fingers caused by the nicotine

❖ When you walk out of a pub or restaurant, and have to walk through smokers stood immediately outside the exit

❖ Smoking in front of children

❖ The smell of smoke on peoples clothes

❖ Walking behind someone who releases a cloud of vapour, which you have no option but to breathe in (and try and guess the flavour)

❖ People who vape in their car, and release a massive smoke cloud out of their window

❖ People walking round with a big vape pipe everywhere they go

❖ People who think they can vape in a No Smoking area

❖ Vapour shops in the high street which always seem empty

Tattoos

- ❖ Self performed tattoos

- ❖ Misspelt tattoos

- ❖ Poor quality tattoos

- ❖ Tattoos on a face or head

- ❖ Tattoos on a neck

- ❖ Football team badge tattoos on the leg

- ❖ Poor quality tattoo parlours being able to operate

- ❖ Tattoo parlours who tattoo under-age people

- ❖ Tattoos on show that should be hidden

- ❖ Tattoos on old people (apart from those in the war)

- ❖ Tattoos that become worse to look at as people get older

- ❖ Young people who still do not consider that a tattoo is forever

Transport

❖ People who use their mobile phones in cars

❖ People who play music too loudly in their car

❖ People who have a hands-free phone in their car, but you can hear the conversation from outside

❖ People with large 4-wheel drive vehicles who will never seem to have more than 2 people in the car

❖ People with large 4-wheel drive vehicles who don't live anywhere that requires the use of the 4-wheel drive option

❖ People who do not acknowledge you when you let them through or let them out of a junction

❖ When a warning light appears on the car dashboard

❖ The time spent filling a vehicle with petrol

❖ People who only use a petrol pump that is the side of the petrol cap

❖ Cars that use the bus lane

❖ Motorists who use their horn unnecessarily

❖ Drivers who don't let you out of a side road, despite them being stationary

❖ Cycle lanes that come to an abrupt end

❖ People who walk past a Pedestrian Crossing and press the button for fun to stop traffic, but have no intention of crossing the road

❖ People who drive on the hard shoulder of a motorway, in order to reach the next exit junction quicker

❖ Expensive food, drink and fuel at motorway services

WEDDINGS

❖ When the Wedding Invitation includes a list of Wedding Presents to buy

❖ Feeling that you have to go to a wedding of a distant relative that you haven't seen for years and hardly know

❖ Waiting ages in the church for the bride to arrive

❖ A very long church service

❖ Children getting bored during the wedding ceremony and making noises or crying

❖ Having to pretend to sing along to the hymns by 'lip syncing', and hoping that nobody spots it

❖ When nobody joins in with the hymns

❖ Having to join in and pose for the wedding photos

❖ The time it takes for the wedding photos to be taken

❖ Waiting to get that first drink

- ❖ Tacky decor at the Wedding Reception

- ❖ Spotting that the Wedding Reception Table Plan has put you on a table with complete strangers

- ❖ Having to make polite conversation with strangers

- ❖ Pretending to be interested in other people's conversations

- ❖ Best Man speeches that are embarrassing and not funny

- ❖ The Bride and Groom being over the top and unrecognisable from their normal selves

- ❖ Mother and Mother-in-law competing to look the best

- ❖ The presenting of flowers and gifts to everyone who helped with the wedding

- ❖ The gap between the Afternoon Reception and the Evening Reception

- ❖ The bar at the Evening Reception only having 2 bartenders to look after over 100 guests

- ❖ Having to watch the Bride and Groom's first dance

- ❖ A DJ playing an awful selection of music

- ❖ Being forced to join in on the dance floor to songs like "YMCA", "Agadoo", "Dancing Queen" etc.

- ❖ Children taking over the dance floor

- ❖ Having to stop the evening to wave off the Bride and Groom

- ❖ That once the Bride and Groom have departed, then that is basically the end of the evening as most people will leave then

- ❖ Thinking that for many couples now, it is highly unlikely that their marriage will survive

WORK COLLEAGUES

❖ Colleagues who moan about everything

❖ Colleagues who moan about the organisation, yet never leave or make a positive contribution

❖ Colleagues always blaming somebody else, and never looking at what they could have done better themselves

❖ Colleagues who regularly take sick days off, but aren't really ill

❖ Colleagues who do the bare minimum and add no extra value

❖ Colleagues who have their own 'agenda' at work

❖ Colleagues who 'fiddle' their timesheets

❖ Colleagues who don't stop talking

❖ Colleagues who interrupt you for a social chat, despite them knowing that you are really busy, and they then go home leaving you to work late to finish up

❖ Colleagues moaning that their "PC is slow"

- ❖ When you and a colleague perform the same role, yet you always seem to do more work

- ❖ Colleagues who eat food in the office that has a strong smell

- ❖ Colleagues who manage to have a "Clear Desk"

- ❖ Colleagues who have a really untidy desk

- ❖ Colleagues with photos of their loved ones on their desk

- ❖ Colleagues who put stickers on their work PC/ laptop

- ❖ Colleagues who don't say hello when they arrive at work in the morning

- ❖ Colleagues who don't say goodbye / goodnight when they leave work in the evening

- ❖ Colleagues who don't turn up at meetings, despite them accepting invitations

- ❖ Colleagues who turn up late for meetings

- ❖ Colleagues who never do the 'tea run', yet always accept others doing it

- ❖ Colleagues who arrive in the office really early, then sarcastically say "Good afternoon" to other colleagues who arrive just after them, and then they leave first at the end of the day

❖ Colleagues who use too many TLAs (Three Letter Acronyms) in the office, and assume that everybody knows what they are referring to

❖ Colleagues who use jargon, such as "Let's Touch Base, Step Up To The Plate, You're On Point, Let's Engage, Going Forward, Thinking Outside The Box, Blue-sky Thinking, Singing From The Same Hymn Sheet, No 'I' In Team, No Brainer, On The Same Page etc."

❖ Colleagues who use Emojis on emails

❖ Colleagues who put a kiss at the end of an email

My List Of Pet Hates

❖

❖

❖

❖

❖

❖

❖

❖

❖

❖

❖

❖

❖

❖

❖

❖

My List Of Pet Hates

- ❖
- ❖
- ❖
- ❖
- ❖
- ❖
- ❖
- ❖
- ❖
- ❖
- ❖
- ❖
- ❖
- ❖
- ❖
- ❖

Printed in Poland
by Amazon Fulfillment
Poland Sp. z o.o., Wrocław

49159240R00036